MW00901812

I would like to dedicate this book to all the young philanthropists who have devoted countless hours and energy to Colonial Kids for a Cause, a lemonade stand started 10 years ago by my four boys—George, Thomas, Henry, William—and their neighborhood friends. To date, they have raised over $400,000 and tons of awareness for local organizations. You are my hero, "LemonAid Kids"! To each and every one of you, my sincerest and hardiest of thanks. You have all richly blessed me and countless others in our wonderful city of Fort Worth.

Love,
Mrs. Marlow

I also would like to dedicate this story to my partners in crime for all things LemonAid and Life. They are those friends who just make living better. They inspire me, they encourage me, and they make me a stronger woman of faith. They also make me a better wife, mother, daughter, and friend. I love you, Julie Diamond and Jan Hurn. Cheers to more sticky hot days ahead!

Love,
Michelle

Celebrating a DecAid of LemonAid Recipients

Susan G. Komen Foundation, United States Military Care Packages, Team Nolan, The First Tee, Cook Children's Medical Center—Teen Room, Wish With Wings, Cook Children's Medical Center—Sit Stay Play, Therapy Dog Program, KinderFrogs at TCU, TCU Starpoint School, and The Gary Patterson Foundation

www.mascotbooks.com

L is for Lemonade

©2019 Michelle McKee Marlow and Cynthia Marlow. All Rights Reserved.
No part of this publication may be reproduced, stored in a retrieval
system or transmitted in any form by any means electronic, mechanical,
or photocopying, recording or otherwise without the permission of the
author.

For more information, please contact:
Mascot Books
620 Herndon Parkway, Suite 320
Herndon, VA 20170
info@mascotbooks.com

Library of Congress Control Number: 2019903741

CPSIA Code: PRT0719A
ISBN-13: 978-1-64307-559-4

Printed in the United States

A Series of
HARD-TO-PRONOUNCE LETTERS

L *is for* LEMONADE

Michelle McKee Marlow
and Cynthia Marlow

Illustrations by Megan Skeels

Luke can say S and R but he cannot say the L sound. When he tries to say an L sound it comes out like W. Instead of saying, "My name is Luke," it sounds like, "My name is Wuke."

There are so many L sounds in the world. Luke sees them everywhere he looks. He sees L at the beginning of words.

LIBRARY. LAUNDROMAT. LUNCHROOM.

He sees L in the middle of words.

ESCALATOR. ALLIGATOR. TRAMPOLINE.

He even sees L at the end of words.

PENCIL. APPLE. TOOL.

The shape of the L is simple. Just two lines. *L looks like a lovely letter,* he thinks. In his mind these words sound just the way they're supposed to, but no matter what he does, Luke cannot say L.

Sometimes Luke feels embarrassed that he has a hard time saying his own name. His mom and dad tell him every night how much they love him. They tell him he's wonderful just the way he is. Luke believes them, but he still wants to learn how to say L like other people. Then he could say "I love you" back to them.

Luke is feeling extra worried this week because in five days he is going to be working at the LemonAid Stand. It's a very special lemonade stand that was created by his friend William, his three older brothers, and all the neighborhood kids.

Every summer, the brothers sell lemonade and cookies to people in town for the big golf tournament. Then, they donate the money they make to different groups in the community. When William turned seven, he got to help his brothers at the stand. This year, Luke is finally old enough to help too!

The morning of the golf tournament, Luke is excited when he sees George, Thomas, and Henry at the LemonAid Stand. He can't wait to help them sell lemonade. This year, the money they make will go to the children's hospital.

Luke is also nervous. Last night, he practiced phrases to say to customers that don't require him to say the letter L. "Here is your drink." "Enjoy your cookies!" "Thank you for donating!"

William gives Luke his royal blue LemonAid shirt. Luke proudly puts it on and watches as William shows him how to arrange the pitchers and the trays of cookies. While they are working, they see something very funny nearby. A dog is wearing a royal blue shirt that matches their shirts!

"This is LuLu," says the lovely woman holding LuLu's lavender leash. "And my name's Lynda. Can you say hi to LuLu?"

"Hi doggie," Luke says. He doesn't want the nice lady to hear him say "WuWu." He doesn't even want to say his name. Luke looks down at his shoes.

"You seem shy," Lynda says. "That's okay. I see you're working at the LemonAid Stand. I love how the brothers donate what they make to different places in the community. LuLu is a therapy dog and loves to go out into the community too. Her favorite place to visit is the children's hospital."

Luke smiles and pats LuLu's head. *What a special dog,* he thinks.

Then Lynda says, "Will you hold LuLu's leash for a few minutes? I forgot her water dish in the car."

Luke smiles and takes the leash as Lynda walks away.

"Hi!" says LuLu.

"You're a dog!" Luke laughs. "Dogs can't talk."

"I can," says LuLu. "I speak dog and I speak people. *Ruff, ruff!* Hello! You know my name. What's yours?"

Luke looks down again. "*Wuke,*" he says quietly.

"Wuke is a nice name," says LuLu.

"It's not *Wuke,*" says Luke. "I just can't say the L sound."

"Ah!" says LuLu. "I met a lovely lady once who taught me a trick for this very thing! When I told her my name, she told me that when she was a girl she couldn't pronounce the L sound either. Then she taught me the trick. Want me to teach you? We're going to need peanut butter!"

"Oh yes *pwease!*" says Luke. "I have a peanut butter sandwich packed for *wunch!* It's at the *WemonAid* Stand." Luke hangs his head when he says *WemonAid.*

"It's okay, Luke!" says LuLu. "I used to only be able to say *woof, woof* instead of *ruff, ruff*. I had to learn some tricks, too!"

Luke comes back with some peanut butter on a spoon.

"When I do tricks my human rewards me with peanut butter," explains LuLu. "But that's not the kind of trick I'm talking about. The trick starts by putting a little peanut butter behind your top front teeth, near the roof of your mouth. Go ahead and try it now."

Luke puts the peanut butter behind his top front teeth. He pushes his tongue up to lick the peanut butter. "LLL..." he says softly as he licks. "LLL.."

He gets a little more peanut butter and tries again. "WuWu..." he says. Then "WuLu." Finally, still softly, he says, "LuLu, LuLu, LuLu." Then he shouts, "LULU!!!"

"Hooray!" LuLu cheers.

Next Luke tries his name.

"Wuuuuu, wuuuuu,

LUUUUUKE!

LEMONADE!

I AM LUKE

AND I LOVE

LEMONADE!"

That day, Luke serves two hundred cups of lemonade. When the customers say thank you, he says, "You're welcome!" Sometimes the L still sounds like a W. But he gets better every time he practices.

The best part is that Luke and his friends raise lots of money for the children's hospital. Luke knows LuLu will love that.

"LuLu!" Luke shouts at the end of the day. "Thank you! I LOVE you!"

"*Ruff, ruff!*" says LuLu, wagging her tail. "You did it! You learned the trick!"

"I did!" says Luke. "I LEARNED it! I LOVE it!"

Michelle **M** _Cynthia_

August 23, 1996 was a special day indeed! Michelle McKee married George Scott Marlow. One of the greatest gifts she received was his sister, Cynthia Ann Marlow. Not only did their sisterhood grow, Michelle shared her love of Speech Language Pathology with Cynthia. Three years later, Cynthia graduated with a Master's in Communication Sciences and Disorders. Since then, both women have become prolific in their field. Michelle, a graduate of TCU, bleeds purple! Her passion for her private practice in Fort Worth has led her to work with hundreds of children aged birth to high school with speech and language impairments. Cynthia, who has a strong sense of adventure, has taken her skills all over the world, including cities such as Monaco, Hong Kong, Bangkok, Gstaad, and Dallas where she has been the Head of Special Education, a Speech Pathologist, and led professional development seminars for several international schools.

Together, their dream for A Series of Hard-To-Pronounce Letters is not to replace a Speech Pathologist, but for the books to be read for pleasure and building confidence in children and students. They are not alone in what they are facing each day. Thank you for joining Michelle and Cynthia on their journey as they continue publishing books that come with "secret tips" to tackle speech and language disorders, and most importantly, bring smiles along the way!